Puffin Books

THI   R

The Tail of the Trinosaur was Charles Causley's first ever story for children and it has now become a classic of narrative verse. The tale of the amazing trinosaur, of how it is brought to the quiet town of Dunborough and what happens next, is a hilarious story that all children will love.

When the trinosaur wakes from its ninety million year sleep, it's not too happy to find itself in the heart of an English town rather than the Amazon Jungle. And once a trinosaur is upset, it's very difficult to know how to calm it down again!

Charles Causley is one of Britain's most distinguished poets. He was born in Launceston, Cornwall, and has spent most of his life there, teaching for many years and then retiring to write full time. He has won many literary awards and prizes, including the Queen's Gold Medal for Poetry.

Also by Charles Causley

Charles Causley

The Tail of the Trinosaur

A story in rhyme
illustrated by Jill Gardiner

Puffin Books

PUFFIN BOOKS

Published by the Penguin Group
Penguin Books Ltd, 27 Wrights Lane, London W8 5TZ, England
Viking Penguin, a division of Penguin Books USA Inc.
375 Hudson Street, New York, New York 10014, USA
Penguin Books Australia Ltd, Ringwood, Victoria, Australia
Penguin Books Canada Ltd, 2801 John Street, Markham, Ontario, Canada L3R 1B4
Penguin Books (NZ) Ltd, 182–190 Wairau Road, Auckland 10, New Zealand

Penguin Books Ltd, Registered Offices: Harmondsworth, Middlesex, England

First published by Brockhampton Press Ltd 1972
Published in Puffin Books 1990
10 9 8 7 6 5 4 3 2

Text copyright © Charles Causley, 1972
Illustrations copyright © Brockhampton Press Ltd, 1972
All rights reserved

Printed in England by Clays Ltd, St Ives plc
Filmset in Baskerville

The Tail of
the Trinosaur
is told in
24 shakes

to
Frances and Carey Tolchard

Shake 1

In Dunborough town
  On the River Drown
    One morning in mild September,

On a day as fair
  Over Guildhall Square
    As anyone could remember,

While the folk all went
  On their business bent
    As they had since the days of the Briton,

And the cows all chewed
  And the pigeons cooed
    As when Domesday Book was written,

A VEHICLE bright
  With flashing light
    – To sirens screaming like a banshee –

Through the South Gate scraped
  As the people gaped
    And cried, excitedly, '*Can* she?'

And from Plymouth Dock
  As the Town Hall clock
    Emitted its usual quarter

There braked in the Square
  With a squeak of air
    A perfectly
        vast
          TRANSPORTER.

With a wondering sound
  As the crowds surged round
    It was plainer
        and plainer
          and plainer

That they couldn't decide
  Just what was inside
    The simply
        e n o r m o u s
          CONTAINER.

Shake 2

Then out of the cab swung the driver's mate
    Like an act at an open-air gala,
And the crowd gave a cheer that the Mayor could hear
    As he polished his chain in his Parlour.
'Dear me!' said His Worship. 'What *is* going on?
    I'd best put on my regalia,
For it might, by a fluke, be a Royal Duke
    Or a visiting Mayor from Australia.'

Up the Town Hall steps ran the driver's mate
    As the townsfolk tittled and tattled,
And he drew from his coat a delivery-note
    And the knocker he loudly rattled.
'Who's there?' said the Mayor as he opened the door
    By its medieval handle,
Then his jaw he dropped and his eyes he popped
    In the manner of a Roman candle.

For there THE MIGHTY TRANSPORTER stood
    And over the people towered,
Quite blocking the scene from the Castle Green
    To the bar of the 'Admiral Howard'.
And the Mayor (as he signed) looked quite nonplussed
    And claimed it was all a bungle.
'But it's marked on the freight,' said the driver's mate.
    'A PRESENT FROM THE AMAZON JUNGLE.'

Now the crate it stood a haystack high
    And its length was a hundred metres
And the Mayor turned as grey as a seaman may
    When he's gone and lost his neaters.*

Just as nobody knew just what to do
    And the children's lips looked quivery,

* A ration of neat rum.

Right up to the Mayor

                    drove

                            Postman Dare

With an air-mail,

              SPECIAL DELIVERY!

For a moment His Worship stood dumb and still

   As a stone Egyptian pharaoh,

Then he scratched his poll, said 'Bless my soul –

   It's

      a

         letter

            from

RIO DE JANEIRO.'

And a curious hush in quite a rush

   Fell over the whole assembly

As the Mayor began the letter to scan,

   His fingers distinctly trembly.

Then his frown was gone and his face it shone

   With a smile so reassuring,

And he said, 'Such a tale I'll now unveil

   As will send your spirits soaring,

Telling all and one of a Dunborough son

   In a lonely jungle-station,

And his GIFT of renown to his old HOME-TOWN

   That will make it the ENVY of the NATION.'

He could hardly hide a tear of pride

   And a couple of noisy swallows,

Then with manly zest he expanded his chest

   And read out the letter

                    as follows.

Mr Mayor,

As I sit in my cabin so small
on the banks of the Amazon River Where
green anacondas through forests crawl And
incredible butterflies shiver, Where boa constrictors
hang down from the trees On branches both
lower and upper To give the unwary a bit of a
squeeze And swallow him slowly for supper: As
high all around the brazil-wood ride The busy
humming-birds hurtle And there glitter and glide
on the evening tide The alligator and turtle Where
a million monkeys from bough to bough Like
woolly birds are zooming, And the jaguar trots
all covered in spots, And orchids rare are blooming;
When I've fried for my supper as evening falls
A plate of steak-armadillo, And my coffee is
drunk and I fall on my bunk — as soon as my
head's on the pillow, I dream every night of the
days long ago When Dunboro Town I would
wander, Never thinking one day I'd be far, far
away Exploring the Great Out Yonder. And when

I remember the deeds that I've done (To admit
it I'd once have been warier) It seems to me I
was certainly THE Most horrible boy in the area.
For I poured dirty water down Widow Brown's
flue, Dressed her donkey in silks and in satins,
And I painted each pew in the church with glue
One day before choral matins.

It was I who set fire to the robes of the choir
From the trebles right down to the basses, And the
water supply I coloured with dye On the day
of the Swimming Club Races. My collection of
fleas to the jumble sale I sent in a box
marked "Havanas", And I hung for a lark the
trees in the park With bunches of stolen bananas.

I filled up the seat of the magistrate's chair
With holly and thistles and prickles, And the lily-
white coat of the rectory goat I painted with
hammers and sickles.

But a time came at last when my boyhood was
past And those crimes in my throat they were
sticking, My remorse it was deep, I was losing my
sleep And my conscience was constantly pricking.
So a gift I decided to send to them all By which

they'd remember me sweetly, And I hunted
the points of the compass about For something
to fill the bill neatly, And imagine my pride (I'd
rejected the hide Of a mammoth and also a dino-
saur) When with fortune unique I found stuck
up a creek The world's weirdest wonder.

a trinosaur!

As above me it leered I confess it appeared To be
not only living but kicking, And I haven't a
doubt that my eyes were both out Of my head with
astonishment sticking, For there's not much I've
missed as a naturalist In my travels to pole and
equator, But I solemnly swear of a creature so
rare I was never before the spectator. For millions of
years in the swamp it had laim More or less in the
same old position, All covered in goo of a horrible hue
That had kept it in splendid condition. Why, it scarcely
seemed dead! From its tail to its head It was perfect
in every feature, And in Dunborough's name I at
once staked a claim On that

truly
remarkable
creature.

So with tackle and with crane From the
place where it had lain We lifted it, as careful
as could be, And one Sunday afternoon On
a sort of a pontoon It was floated down the
river to the sea.
    And the savage Indian tribes, Coffee-planters
and their wives In amazement held their hands
up to the sky As they stood upon the shore And
they saw that trinosaur Just like an ocean-
liner pass them by.
    Now the size of this strange figure Was a circus-
tent's - or bigger - Though its stem and stern were
infinitely slender. Down its spine, like sugar-lu—
Ran a single row of bumps, Thus denoting that it
was of female gender. And it had a pair of eyes
Each a dustbin-lid in size In a head that wa—
the size of a small barque.
    ("Oh I'm glad," cried more than one, "suc—
monster's dead and gone, For I wouldn't

16

5/ to meet it after dark!") It had most un-
pleasant claws And the hungriest of jaws That
were ever seen in continent or ocean, But the
most astounding feature of this antiquated
creature Was its most _amazing mode of loco-
motion_.

There were two legs at the front But its rear
was rather _blunt_ And was quite devoid of
limbs in every way, And it would have _scraped
the floor_ And have made the trino sore Had its
tail not acted as a prop and stay.

So with many a start and stop, Half a leap
and half a hop, It had pranced around in prehistoric climes, Though the reason's pretty clear Why it grew
extinct, I fear, For it simply hadn't travelled with
the times.

When it reached the city docks It was packed in
such a box — The largest ever from the naval store —
That a thousand dockyard-maties cried, "We don't

17

6/

know WHAT that freight is For we've
never seen the like of it before!"

Then they lashed it to a raft Of considerable draught And with a pair of tow-
ropes quite gigantic They secured it to
the stern Of the tug known as <u>The Tern</u>
That hauled it clean across the loud
Atlantic.

When I heard (while down in Chile)
It had reached the Isles of Scilly I at
once put pen to paper with its story,
For to reach its destination With no
word of explanation Would have
caused a fearful fuss and a furore.

Now to Dunborough and its folks,
To make up for my bad jokes, This

trinosaur, in recompense, I send; And
it comes with Love from one who prefers
to be anon. Which is why he simply

signs himself

A Friend

Shake 5

So with hammer and chisel and mallet and crow
    They cautiously cracked the container – and oh
With terror some trembled and awe they all cried
    When they first caught a glimpse of the creature inside.

From the tip of its tail to the top of its head
    They'd never seen anything like it, they said.
'We know,' cried the workmen, 'its life is long done,
    But it's all we can do not to down tools and run!'

Said the Mayor, 'Though it means that the rates are increased,
    We *must* build a Suitable Home for the beast
– As in London and New York and Paris you see 'em –
    A Dunborough Natural History Museum.

And before you said Alderney, Guernsey or Sark
    (Or Jersey, for that) down at Priory Park
The lorries arrived and the builders began
    On Sir Archibald Architrave's prize-winning plan.

The roof was a bubble that spun round about,
    The walls slanted inwards, the windows leaned out.
With colours astonishing it was a-shine,
    And practically everyone thought it divine.

But old Grannie Penney who lived by the river
    Said, 'Something about the place gives me a shiver.
That silly old kickshaw I simply can't bide
    Any more than the monster they're putting inside.

'I can't see the church-yard, it's ruined my view,
    My lights are all blocked and I think I shall sue,
My cat has had kittens, my dog's having fits,
    And the nerves of my budgie are bothered to bits.

'Quite up with that building I really am fed,
    It's more like a tumbledown aeroplane shed.
I'll move to my sister's in Abergavenny
    If fate don't move first,' grumbled old Grannie Penney.

'Each time that I shake out a duster or mat
   That beast makes me come over funny, that's flat.
And night after night when I go to my bed
   It seems to be *staring right at me*,' she said.

'I don't like the look that it's got in its eye
   (Although it's a dead 'un) – I just don't know why.
That creature means trouble! You'll all rue the day!'
   Said old Grannie Penney, '*so mark what I say.*'

Shake 6

BUT –

The hammers they rang
  And the saws they sang
    As the builders went through their paces,

And the steel and the glass
  Fairly jumped off the grass
    And into the proper places.

They struggled with struts
  And they juggled with nuts,
    And they bolted and braced and cleated,

Till at last with a cheer
(And a barrel of beer)
It was
    Absolutely
        finally
            completed.

And right in the middle
    Stood the green and grinning trinosaur,
Its eye and coat a-gleaming
    As if it was in its prime,
For they'd scrubbed it
    And polished it
    As fine as you or I e'er saw
Till gone was every single speck
    Of tropic mud and slime.

Its shiny tail was slippery
   (You could have made a slide of it)
And imitation jungle trees
   Were built with finest art,
With lots of central heating
   At the front and back and side of it
To keep the creature cosy
   So it wouldn't fall apart.

And the Mayor and Corporation
　　Very early took their station
　　　　(Robed and ermined) as determined
　　　　　By the Dunborough Town Clerk,

And behind the Borough banner
In a very stately manner
    They proceeded in procession
        To the site on Priory Park.

There were guests — at least a score —
    And their morning coats they wore,
        Also shiny toppers, silver ties and spats,

And their wives (with spacious smiles)
    In the very latest styles,
        That included most extraordinary hats.

There was scarlet Admiral Bounty
   – Lord Lieutenant of the County –
      There were brownie guides and cub scouts standing steady,

And officials large and small
  Who'd come down from County Hall,
    And the Fire Brigade with engine at the ready.

As the Band made an assault on
  'Orb and Sceptre' (William Walton)
And a set of variations
  On 'The Bonnie Brier Bush',

Crowds and crowds of people muttered,
And the flags and banners fluttered,
  And the children got all cluttered,
And their parents murmured,
        'Ssh!'

While within its cabin glassy
   (Hidden, head and tail and chassis)
    As if waiting for its moment
     Stood the scaly trinosaur,

And they had a piece of string
   Which when pulled they hoped would bring
    The giant flag that covered it
     Completely
        to
        the
        f
        l
        o
        o r.

Meanwhile from St. Mary's tower
　　From a very early hour
　　　　The ringers sounded out a happy peal,
And in accents proud, the Mayor
　　Said, 'This building I declare
　　　　Is quite open, and my joy I can't conceal.'

Then he pressed a little switch
　　And without the slightest hitch
　　　　As the sort of silence fell one can't ignore,

Down the covers fell so neat
From its head right to its feet
And revealed to all the world
THE
TRINOSAUR.

Shake 7

For a moment rare
They looked at it there
With its antique glance
And its three-pronged stance,
And from hill to hill
All the folk stood still
As the trino vast
From the living past
Seemed to stare
   And glare
     And leer
       And peer
         And glint
           And squint
  Both here and there
From its crystal lair.

Though its head not a mite
  Moved to left nor right,

Its eye seemed to follow you
    Everywhere
With expression strange
That seemed to change
  With the shifting
    Drifting
  Light of day.

And it looked at them all
  As if to say,
'Good afternoon –
  I'm yesterday.'

Shake 8

But the Mayor, Mayoress and party,
  (Appetites distinctly hearty)
    Soon recovered their composure once again,

With their nervous systems doubly
  Fortified by lots of bubbly
    As the waiters handed everyone champagne.

With a sip and then a nibble
  Lord Elastic, Lady Sybil,
    And the others chattered like the monkeys do.

You and I'd not like to be 'em
  In that trinosaur museum
    As it hotter
    hotter
    hotter
    hotter grew.

But it wasn't the bubbly
(As some people vowed)
It wasn't all the fancy clothes,
It wasn't the crowd.

It wasn't the weather
(Though it WAS a trifle trying),
Nor Bill the boiler-man who sent
The temperature high-skying.

It was hotter than Vesuvius
    Hotter than the sand,
      Hotter than the sun
        In a southern land;

Hotter than the red rocks
    Underneath the sea,
      Hotter than the jungle
        Where the trino used to be.

It wasn't Billy Boiler's fault
    The switches all stuck.
      He stood and scratched his sorry head,
    Said,
    'Just
    my
    luck.'

Shake 9

But little Sammy Smother
    Who was standing with his mother
        Just outside the town museum at the time,

Was emitting little cries of
    Joy at all the wheres and whys of
        The great trino as it stood there so sublime,

When quite suddenly he gasped
    And his mother's hand he clasped,
        And in manner hushed and horrified he said,

'I don't *think* that I'm mistaken
    – And I'm feeling rather shaken –
        But I'm SURE I saw the MONSTER MOVE its HEAD!'

'Sammy Smother,' said his ma,
  'It's a wicked boy you are
    Trying hard to spread such panic and confusion —'

'Bless my soul!' said little Sam,
  'It's just winked an eye now, mam.
    I just KNOW it AIN'T an OPTICAL ILLUSION.'

And it wasn't said in fun,
  For the trino had begun
    In all that extra heating to revive,

And the rather special clay
  Of the jungle where it lay
    Had preserved it
      NINETY MILLION YEARS
        ALIVE!

Shake 10

The ceiling

                  shivered

The floor-boards

                  quivered

The boiler

                  belched

And the nuts all

                  squelched

The stairs were

                  smashed

And the pebbles

                  dashed

The carpets

                  rumpled

And the concrete

                  crumpled

The balloons all

                  popped

And the flags all

                  flopped

And shocked and

                  shattered

The people

      S C A T T E R E D

As the whole town

         rang

        With a

        crash

        CRASH

        BANG!

Shake 11

Folk were filled with such surprise
   They could scarce believe their eyes
      (If they hadn't seen it they'd have needed proof)

And they turned distinctly pale
   As the trino wagged its tail
      And removed (quite accidentally) the roof.

As it turned so slowly round
   Several walls fell to the ground
      (One imagines it was feeling rather stiff),

And it flexed a fearsome claw
   And to everybody's awe
      Gave the top of the gasometer a sniff.

Then it drained the waters cool
   Of the Priory Paddling Pool
      And with an ease incredible to see,

Struck the church tower at an angle,
   Made the contents jingle-jangle
      And the venerable clock chime twenty-three.

Through the windows and the doors
.   And the ceiling and the floors
        And the multitude of spaces in between,

Every citizen and guest
    Joined the rout with all the rest
        And retreated in a panic from the scene.

From a distance safe and wise
People watched and rubbed their eyes
At a sight not seen since very long B.C.,

And the beast to Borough Square
  Gave a prehistoric air
    As it chewed up fifty bushes and a tree.

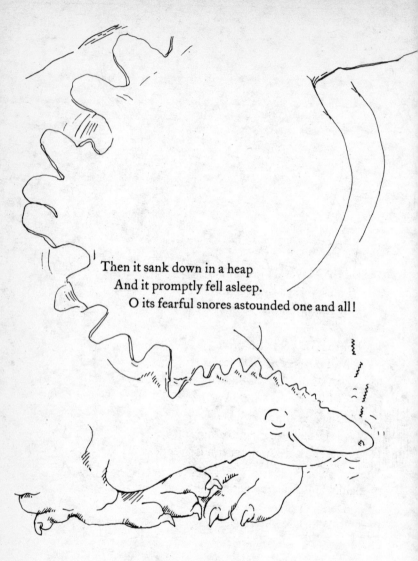

Then it sank down in a heap
And it promptly fell asleep.
O its fearful snores astounded one and all!

(Though the music had no title
It was like a loud recital
On the organ at the Royal Albert Hall.)

Said the Mayor, 'This isn't pretty —
    I must form a small committee
        Till the Services assistance to us send,

'For the Air Force isn't free
    And the Navy's all at sea,
        And the Army's on manoeuvres this weekend.'

So His Worship made his pick,
    Called a meeting double-quick
        At a very secret, hush-hush rendezvous.

Said, 'This situation fierce
    Doesn't call for *volunteers* —
        Which is why I asked for
                you
                    and
                        you
                            and
                                you.'

Shake 12

There was Alastair Disaster
   Once a grammar school headmaster
      And whose Latin verse was said to be inspired,

And Miss Esmeralda Flight
   The well-known toxophilite,
      And Wing Commander Wallaby (Retd).

There was Leading Seaman Noggin
   Who'd been years upon the oggin,*
      Stanley Sparks the Captain of the Fire Brigade.

There was dear old Dr Query
   And his friend Father O'Leary,
      And the local undertaker, Mr Spade.

There was Mrs Wheeler-Bent
   Who had stood for Parliament,
      Walter Wave, who'd swum the Channel rather
      slowly,

Sergeant Stripe (who'd borne and grinned it
   Out in Burma as a Chindit)
      And Bernie Ball, the famous England goalie,

With the landlord, Percy Quart
   Who with guns was quite a sport,
      They assembled in the cellar of 'The Boar',

* The sea

And the air was filled with questions
    And some rather wild suggestions
        When they heard
            a knock
        Like **THUNDER**
            on the door.
They thought it was the trinosaur
The huge and handsome trinosaur
A-knocking on and blocking
(Surely couldn't be *unlocking*?)
In a manner rather shocking
The entrance to their hideaway
(They hoped that it would stride away
Or gracefully would glide away)
A-bumping   grumping   thumping
At their secret cellar door.

But Leading Seaman Noggin
– After just a little sippers* –
    (He'd a bottle with some grog in)

Crept as quietly as quiet
    Like a shadow on a diet
        In his naval-issue slippers

And with not a jar or jolt
Turned the handle, slid the bolt,
Like the others, certain sure
That the knocks they heard before
Were coming from the trino,
From the tri — no — saur.

* Rum

With a simply awful THWACK
Suddenly the door flew back

(Making everybody blench
And their brows with terror drench)

And with somewhat hasty gait
And the words, 'Sorry I'm late,'

Came Professor Cyril Stench
(Chairman of the Local Bench),
Fellow of an Oxford college
And possessing quite a smattering
Of scientific knowledge
(His friends were more than flattering),

Said, 'When I saw the trino
Prancing round just like a rhino
It was clear as clear as clear as clear to see
That the one man in the nation
Who could save a situation
Fast approaching devastation,
And perhaps civilization,
(Please excuse self-commendation)
was
unquestionably,
definitely,
ME.

'So I took a taxi-cab,
Notes I simply had to grab
From a locker in my lab.

Up the stairs with leap and bound!
Scientific studies found!

Observations
Notes
                    and data
All corrections
                    and errata,

And – among them all – HOORAY!

What we need
to

WIN THE DAY.'

Shake 13

See them sitting in a square

Fireman

    bowman

        goalie

           mayor

Doctor

    undertaker

        preacher

Soldier

    sailor

        airman

           teacher

Channel-swimmer,

    Licensee,

        And the would-have-been M.P.,

Following closely as they can
The Professor's MASTER-PLAN.

'My idea,' says the Professor as among his notes he delves,
' Is that those of us in Dunborough should deal with this
    OURSELVES.
We could shoot it as it slept, of course, but that would be barbaric,
We could chase it to the River Drown and sink it like a carrack,

'We could drop a rock upon it from the top of the church tower,
Or send harpoons and javelins and arrows in a shower,
There are COUNTLESS ways UNCIVILIZED — of these I
   need not speak —

'But I feel we should PRESERVE IT, for the creature is unique:
And it seems to me quite obvious that what we have to do
Is to capture and present it to a Very Special Zoo.

'As it slumbers there so sweetly in its grassy green abode — O
I implore you to remember just what happened to the dodo,
And before you're swayed this way or that by military talk,
Fellow citizens, remember the sad fate of the great auk.

SO

'While the trino's sleeping now as deep as in a trance
   We'll try a small experiment

       while we have got the chance!'

Shake 14

'Observe,' the good Professor said,
    'That here I have a phial
Of rather special liquid gas
    I want to put on trial.

'I've only just invented it
    For use in zoos and circuses
Upon ALL KINDS OF ANIMALS
    For VETERINARY purposes.

Supposing you're a hippo with the toothache or the flu,

A hedgehog with the prickly heat,
a jumpy kangaroo,

Queasy quagga in a freighter
or an airborne alligator

Or a jackal with a crackle
or a rather nervous gnu.

'Just imagine it –

a lion with a thousand purple spots

Or a zebra with no dashes

but with quite a lot of dots,

A much-too lively sloth

or a wild-cat from Arbroath

That's a-wailing like the bagpipes
at the Edinburgh Tattoo.

And fancy it – a honey-bear
who's in an awful jam,

A foaming homing-pigeon,
coos, 'I don't know where I am.'

A giraffe with swollen glands
or a camel short of sands,

A cuckoo who can only say
'Tu whit' and then 'Tu whu',

Or a bird who wonders if it's cock-a-one
Or cockatoo.

'For such moments quite distressing
                              I decided it was pressing
To produce a simple remedy
                              Sensationally new,
(Effective, easy, safe AND cheap)
                              to send a creature fast asleep
For anything up to a week
                              and maybe even two.

'And, my friends, only last night
                              As the moon was losing light
And my head was pounding
                              very like a drum,
Round the lab, quite frantic, pacing
                              with my brainbox fairly racing
I was tearing at my hair
                              Absolutely in despair
That the answer I was chasing
                              Wasn't there,

                    WHEN

Just like a flash so bright
                              the solution came in sight
                              as

62

Shake 15

'That this knockout of a gas
        every other will surpass
Is apparent to me
        more and more and more,
Which is why I've brought you some
        in this jolly little drum
That I found in my
        laboratory store.
And I know with joy you'll jump
        at this hose-pipe and this pump
And the chance to try it on
        THE TRINOSAUR.

'According to my many calculations
        you will find
That the gas has NO EFFECT AT ALL
        upon the HUMAN kind,
But I think that I should warn you
        – or we might get in a pickle –
That the trino's hide is touchy
        at the slightest slap or tickle.

So cautiously we'll climb its tail

                    (a very careful track)

And navigate the many bumps

                    we see along its back.

THIS portion of its body

                    has NO FEELING, I declare,

So it's more or less quite certain

                    that it won't know we are there,

And three of us along its spine

                    quite peacefully will pass

With stirrup-pump

            and length of hose

                    and cylinder of gas.

And when we get right to its head

                    of curious shape and size,

Our leader hanging upside-down

                    between its sleeping eyes,

As SOON as we've the SIGNAL

                    from the fellow with the hose

PROFESSOR STENCH'S SWILIUM

                    we'll shoot right up its nose.

'O the trino it will slumber
    And the trino it will snore
Though the Army doesn't get here
    For another month or more.

'And just in case the citizens
    Should fuss and fume and fret
We'll proceed to trap the trino
    Underneath the strongest net.

'And night and day we'll guard it there
    Both lovingly and close
And every time it stirs we'll give it
    Just another dose.

'And when the trino wakens
    And is feeling good as new
We'll present it with the freedom
    Of the latest,
        greatest,
            zoo.'

Shake 16

Plan you gave us —

bound to save us —

You're a wonder!

cried the Mayor.

Said mine host,

Don't want to boast —

Always thought

you'd brains to spare.

Said Miss Flight,

How very *bright!*

Soldier,

Boys, we've got it made!

It's a clicker,

said the vicar.

Very deep,

said Mr Spade.

Man's a master,

said Disaster.

Super duper.

(Wheeler-Bent),

Rich and rare, man,

said the airman,

And the swimmer,

Heaven-sent!

Agree wholly!

called the goalie,

Said the Doctor,

It's five-star!

Oh what larks!

cried Fireman Sparks,

And *Splice the mainbrace!*

piped Jack Tar.

Shake 17

No delaying (needs no saying)
    Each one volunteers his aid.
'Not a doubt,' says the Professor,
    Of such stuff are heroes made.

'But the spear-head of the Oper-
    Ation Trinc calls for three.
Therefore, Fireman Sparks, ex Leading Seaman
      Noggin
    FOLLOW ME.'

One with pump and one with hose-pipe,
    One with cylinder of gas,
Tip-toed up to where the trino
    Snored as if its lungs were brass.

On the way they found a ladder
    Lying by a garden wall.
Now they've neared the Sports Pavilion!
    Through the hedge-gap see them crawl!

On the creature's rear advancing
Party takes a steady course,
Through the buttercups and daisies
And *a patch of prickly gorse*.

All the citizens of Dunborough
  To their houses were confined,
Though some squinted through a shutter
  Or a chink in window-blind,

While concealed behind the gas-works
  Stood the Mayor and his crew
Armed with nets and pegs and mallets,
  All prepared to die (or do).

Now the trio leans the ladder
  Gently on the trino's tail.
('Never thought I'd,' Fireman Sparks sighed,
  'Ever work on such a scale.')

As the trino they're ascending,
    Wriggling from bump to bump,
'Blowed if this,' says Seaman Noggin,
    'Don't give me the blooming hump.'

And the watchers in amazement
   Looks incredulous exchange,
As they see the careful climbers
   On the living mountain-range.

Underneath them in its slumber
   – Undisturbed by jig or jog –
Trino sounds like ship on Humber
   Snoring homeward through the fog.

Now the Fireman's hanging downwards
    – O what dizziness he feels! –
While above him the Professor
    Holds him tightly by the heels.

(Hanging upside-down between its
    Eyes of very ancient hue,
Fireman can't forbear to wonder
    If it wakes just what he'll do.)

Noggin's pumping! Gas goes thumping!
    (All is well, the trio thinks.)
Says Professor, 'Trino – bless her –
    Out for 40,000 winks.

'When its breath comes slow – then slower
    – Very close watch we must keep –
Is the sign the trino's sinking
        Into
            deep
                and
                    deeper
                        sleep.'

But – mistake in calculation –
    – Poor Professor was aghast –
For instead of breathing slower
    Trino now was breathing fast.

Breathing quick and ever quicker
    Till it gave a loud
                        HICCOUGH!
'Mercy me', exclaimed Professor,
    'But I think it's waking up!'

'Great sea-cats!' called Seaman Noggin,
    'But I'm certain sure that I'll
Soon be wishing I was missing
    From the back of this reptile.'

'Found the reason!' cried Professor.
    'Dreadful error I behold!
SWILIUM FOR *WARM-BLOODED*
    CREATURES!
    AND THE TRINOSAUR'S IS
                COLD!'

'Gas – cold-blooded creatures – wakens
– Plan abandoned – fearful flaw!
Seems to me it would be best to
Rather rapidly WITHDRAW.'

Shake 18

Then all at once the trinosaur
Emitted just the kind of roar
You might have thought had echoed o'er
Some distant prehistoric shore:

Though scholars great and scholars small
Insist such creatures NEVER bawl
Or even as an infant squall
Or make the slightest sound at all –

The fact remains that up till then
The beast was quite beyond the ken
Of scientific modern men,

Who understandably would hum
And say, 'OF COURSE the creature's dumb'

Or on the other hand may haw
And say, 'It's silent, we're quite sure.'

But this conclusion was absurd
In Dunborough
Where its cry
WAS HEARD.

And hear it did our heroes three
As through the town for all to see
Professor, Fireman, Jolly Jack —
Away they galloped on its back.

Yes – off went the trinosaur
     and through the little town it tore
    Just like a puppy off a lead in great exhilaration;
It whirled and waved its tail about,
     (you should have seen it flail about!)
    A-flattening the fir-trees in the Dunborough
     Plantation.

There simply was no stopping it,
     The gallant three still topping it,
    As on the Borough Bowling Green it left a giant
     spoor.
And oh it hopped and skipped and jumped,
     against the Castle wall it bumped
    And made it more a ruin than it ever was before.

Shake 19

It scattered cows,
    It scattered swine,
        It chased a goods-train up the line
            And through the supermarket took a stroll.

On the Castle Green it wandered
    And it chewed the Borough Standard
        As it fluttered on a newly-painted pole.

And the trino seemed QUITE GLUM
    That nobody else would come
        As it rambled and it gambolled here and there,

So as if to keep its pecker up
        It bent a double-decker up
                That happened to be standing in the Square.

On the practice-room it sat,
        Squashed the instruments all flat
                Of the Borough Silver Jubilee Brass Band,

And as up the hill it sprinted
        In the cinema it squinted
                (It's a blessing that no matinée was planned).

Through the reservoir it splashed
   As the park-attendants dashed
      Like a little herd of goats upon a mountain,

Then it suddenly reversed
   And began to quench its thirst
      In the Victory Illuminated Fountain.

As it gobbled up a snack
   From a rather large haystack
      That down beside the water-meadows lay,

It whistled and it wheezed
    And immediately sneezed
        And blew every single wisp of it away.

Said the Mayor to his platoon,
    'We must take some action soon
        Or those three will think our duty we are shirking,

'For I'm certain and I'm sure
    Riding on that trinosaur
        'S an experience that's really rather irking.'

But suggestions there were none
    (For 'twas simpler said than done)
        And our heroes' chances seemed not worth a dime,

When –
refusing to be baffled –
All three leapt off on a scaffold
That was round the Baptist Chapel at the time.

O you should have heard the cheer
That from Dunborough rang clear
As without a single mutter or a murmur,

That indomitable trio
With considerable brio
Descended once again on terra firma.

'My dear friends,' then said the Mayor,
'You have given us a scare
And we're *so* relieved to see you safely down,

'But one fact I must deplore –
We're just where we were before
With that beast still gallivanting round the town.

'Though the danger won't be ended
Till the trino's apprehended
– And such a task the Army's not afraid of –

'I've the feeling still, I own,
We should deal with it ALONE
And show the world what
DUNBOROUGH
is made of!'

Shake 20

Then all at once Miss Flight
    That well-known toxophilite
      With extraordinary luck
        By a sudden thought was struck
          And with flashing eye and bright
          (Quite a formidable sight)
            Straight before His Worship stood
            Like a female Robin Hood.

Said, 'You have no need, I know,
    Of my arrow and my bow –
      From our vow we cannot swerve
        Such a creature to *Conserve*.
          Though in former days, I'm sure,
            They'd have *Killed* that trinosaur
            It would really be unkind
              Not to *Save* it for *Mankind*.

'Though it seems *Complete* reliance
    Can't be placed on modern *Science*,
      And, I feel, a charm or spell
        Somehow wouldn't work too well,
          Long ago it was habitual
            To perform an *Ancient Ritual*.

'And this often was a saviour –
　　From such dragonish behaviour
　　　　As the flattening of a city
　　　　　　Quite without remorse or pity –
　　　　　　　　Traffic veering – horses rearing –
　　　　　　　　Herds of cattle disappearing –
　　　　　　　　　Pitches generally queering –
　　　　　　　　　　Every single person fearing!

'Possibly,' said Esmeralda
　　As if something strange compelled her,
　　　　'It may prove *No Panacea*
　　　　　　Yet
　　　　　　　　I *think*
　　　　　　　　　　I've an
　　　　　　　　　　　IDEA!'

People thought their ears deceived,
　　Looked incredibly relieved.
　　　　Cried the Mayor, with hope new-springing,
　　　　　　To the very last straw clinging,
　　　　　　　'Dearest madam, be so kind –
　　　　　　　　Tell us what is in your mind.'

　　　　　　　　　'*The Performance of a Rite*',
　　　　　　　　　　Said Miss Esmeralda Flight.

Shake 21

Yes, up spoke Esmeralda Flight
   As boldly as a gun,
Though sixty summers she had seen
   If she had seen but one.

'Although I must confess,' she said,
   'The prospect isn't nice,
Our last resort that beast to thwart
   Is by a *Sacrifice*.

'For I've been told, in days of old,
   They'd calm a monster down
By offering a virgin maid
   That *she* might save a town.

'And after it had chewed her up
   And all its tribute got –
The beast (quite tame) from whence it came
   Returned, as like as not.

'Though from *Appeasement*, on the whole,
   I wish that we forbore –
If it beguiled a *Dragon* wild,
   Why not a trinosaur?'

The Mayor then said, and shook his head,
   'It's very plain to see
Not one you'll find in her right mind
   That sacrifice to be.

'We wouldn't spoil your plan to foil
   The trino cool and clever,
But – let it sup a lady up
   To save our skins?
        Why –
          NEVER.

'And if for want of human flesh
   It thinner gets and thinner,
That beast SHAN'T munch a maid for lunch
   Or breakfast,
       tea,
         or dinner.'

     But clearly Esmeralda Flight
       With this could not agree,
     For she replied with simple pride,
       'That Sacrifice I'll be.

'And I shall dress in lily-white
   And brush and braid my hair,
And bear a posy red and blue
   Upon the morning air.

'A verse or two I'll then recite
   Out of an ancient ode,
And I shall sing an antique song
   That's in the Dorian mode.'

(Then whispered Seaman Noggin, 'Boys,
   Although I ain't no quitter –
I can't conceal this time I feel
   Quite sorry for that crittur.

'When Esmeralda sings and spouts
   And trino frowns above her,
And she draws near in all that gear,
   I think we'd best take cover.')

But though the Mayor and all folk there
    Implored her to relent,
Clear as the sun Miss Esme on
    Self-sacrifice was bent.

'That no-one here's the slightest fear
    Is perfectly well-known,
But – I entreat – that beast *I'll* meet
    And deal with all *alone*.

'So do not flurry, homeward hurry
    With a gentle tread,
And draw the blind, and when you've dined,
    Go early all to bed.

'And bolt the door both aft and fore
    – It really is a must –
And sleep as sound, all eiderdowned,
    As do, I'm told, the just.

'And when my deed of daring's done
    Then let the poets write
She did it all for Dunborough,'
    Said Esmeralda Flight.

Shake 22

But none of the townsfolk
 A morning watch kept
 For the whole population
 It slept and it slept.
 The people they slumbered
 The clock round about
 By all their adventures
 Completely worn out,
 And long after sun-up
 In bed they still lay
 And quite unaware
 Of the dawn of the day.

93

When at the Mayor's mansion
In Dockacre Dell
There sounded a sudden
Great ring on the bell,
And O such a knocking
Was heard on the door
The Mayor from his bed
Almost fell on the floor.
'I'm all of a ferment
And flutter, I swear,'
To the Lady Mayoress
Said His Worship the Mayor.

'That dreadful commotion,'
She said, ' I decry,'
As she slowly and solemnly
Opened an eye.
'Though just what's the reason
I vow and declare
I haven't a notion,
And don't really care.
But I've got a feeling
Disaster's not far.
If you ask my advice
You'll stay right where you are.'

But hard upon the window-pane
  A fist of pebbles flew
    And someone on the knocker beat
    A violent tattoo,
      And loudly as the siren sounds
      Upon the Dunborough Brewery
        They heard a most exasperated
        Cry of female fury.
          At once His Worship recognized
          That tone of voice commanding,
          And like a bolt out of his bed
            Shot straight along the landing.

He hurried swiftly down the stair,
The door he fast unlocked,
He'd only his pyjamas on
But nobody was shocked,
For there with crown of flowers askew
And hair a sorry sight,
And virgin gear in state severe
Stood Esmeralda Flight.
And all about the Square the Mayor
With anxious eye did peer
In case the tricky trinosaur
Was bringing up the rear.

But to his relief
– He could almost have cheered –
Upon the horizon
No trino appeared,
And he cried, 'Dear Miss Flight
From the beast are you fleeing?
Please say that it's you –
Not a ghost that I'm seeing.
From this world I had feared
You were gone in great glory –
Do please come inside
And tell us your story.'

Said Miss Flight then to the Mayor
    As she sank into a chair
    And consumed a cup of coffee
    With a very thankful air,
        'I'd have never guessed a monster
        – O so fickle and so skittish –
            Would behave in such a manner
            So entirely un-British.
                When I found it snoring loudly
                By the Pennygillam Wood
                I approached it very softly
                As tradition says one should.

'But as I stood before it
    In my ribbons and my train,
    It opened up an eye and then
        It Went to Sleep Again.
            And when my verse I chanted
            At the breaking of the dawn,
                It blinked the other eye and gave
                The most tremendous yawn.
                As slowly I gyrated
                At the coming of the day,
                    Its tail it swished as if it wished
                    That I Would Go Away.

'Though long before its jaws I stood
And offered up my flowers,
It took one peep – then fell asleep
For hours and hours and hours,
And when I offered up *Myself*
It gave a sort of shiver
And caught my posy in a claw
And flung it in the river.
And then my sacrificial robe
It seized with fearful grip,
And dumped me very gently
On the Corporation Tip.

'I shouldn't be complaining –
  But oh, it isn't nice
    When such a beast refuses
    A maiden's sacrifice.
      Right to the heart it's cut me
      Like the sharpest kitchen-knife.
        I've never been insulted
        Quite like this *In All My Life*.'
          And O her eye it flashed as bright
          As Longships or Nantucket,
            And then her tears began to fall
            Enough to fill a bucket.

The Mayor and Mayoress hastened
  With their tissues and their hankies
    And the atmosphere resounded
    With their 'Much obliged's and 'Thank'ee's
      As they voiced to Esmeralda
      In her sacrificial vesture
        ALL the thanks of ALL the people
        For her brave and noble gesture.
          'In the whole of Dunborough's history,'
          They said, 'There's none to match you,
            We'll surely need to mark your deed
            By plaque or bust or statue.

'For we thought by now, dear lady,
  You'd have surely been a goner
  Which is why we'll try and do you
    The most special, signal honour.'
      So Esmeralda's spirits rose
      Considerably higher,
        And all around the floor and ground
        Became a little drier.
          'And now,' His Worship said, 'before
          I go completely barmy,
          Just one thing more:
            THAT TRINOSAUR
              WE'RE LEAVING TO THE ARMY.

'And when the troops they come to town
  – In all the world, none better! –
  The trino's skin ain't worth a pin
  (That's if they got my letter).
    In military tactics they'll
    Be anything but lacking,
      And very soon they'll change its tune
      And send that creature packing.
        I say it once, I say it twice,
          – Let none my words be scorning –
          That trinosaur will be no more
            AS OF NEXT MONDAY
            MORNING.'

Shake 23

But early Monday morning
    With the coming of the dawn,
Young Sammy Smother through the town
    Ran crying out,
            'IT'S GAWN!

'I got up very early
    And I searched just everywhere –
I rubbed my eyes! To my surprise
    It simply wasn't there!

'It's been and gone and scarpered
    And it's left us in a funk!
Now who'd have thought the trino
    Would have done a blessed bunk?'

At Sammy's shout the people
    Came springing from their beds,
And from the doors and windows
    Soon were sticking out their heads.

'Oh, it's Sammy!'
                      'Where's your mammy?'
'*What* was that we heard you say?'
'Trino's missing?'
                  'Oh, how spiffing!'
'Just imagine it!'
             'HOORAY!'

And the citizens of Dunborough
   They looked hither, they looked yon,
But they found to their astonishment
   The trinosaur was gone.

It wasn't on the hillside
   And it wasn't on the down,
It wasn't in the meadows
   Down beside the River Drown.

It wasn't in the Priory Park,
   It wasn't in the pool,
It wasn't in the playground
   Of the Church of England school.

Both street and square were free as air
   Of any beast-ly bother,
For in the town it wasn't found
   From one end to the other.

That all the folk were puzzled
   There was not the slightest doubt.
They said, 'This is a mystery
   We really can't make out.'

When,
    'I've got it!' cried Disaster
  (Once headmaster) to the Mayor
(Spoke so sharply that His Worship
   Leapt a little in the air).

'It only now occurred to me
    – The very strangest thing! –
When looking at the calendar –
    Today's the FIRST OF SPRING!

'And on this day the birds and beasts
    – So ancient lore relates –
Go searching here and searching there
    To find themselves their mates.

'And THAT is why the trinosaur
    Is swimming in the foam
From east to west to its love-nest
    Back in its jungle-home.

'Of finding mates in Dunborough
    A trino's not much hope –
It clearly needs a wider sphere
    And somewhat larger scope.'

You should have heard the people
    Make such a hullabaloo!
They hadn't felt so happy
    Since the end of World War II.

They laughed and sang and shouted,
    With joy their faces shone,
To think at last from Dunborough
    The trinosaur had gone.

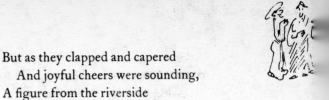

But as they clapped and capered
 And joyful cheers were sounding,
A figure from the riverside
 To Borough Square came pounding.

'Your Worship! Oh, Your Worship!'
 Yelled Sammy Smother's brother
'You know we *lost* one trinosaur?
 Well, now we've got ANOTHER!'

'Such dreadful news,' declared the Mayor,
    'Makes me feel cold and clammy.
Is that the truth he's telling us?
    Please ask young Simmy, Sammy.'

Said Sim, 'That it's a trino
    Is obvious – alack –
And so's the DOUBLE row of bumps
    I saw upon its back.'

'A DOUBLE ROW?' cried Noggin,
    'Why then, it's plain to see:
This time it ain't a female
    But the opposite – a HE.

'And as he's swimming UP the Drown
    – Now don't forget the date! –
He's searching for a partner
    And he's just a little late.

'Although I'll lay with love his eye
    Burns like a lump of cannel,
By fate's sad twist his mate he's missed
    While in the English Channel.'

When to the highest hilltop
    The citizens had sped
They saw the trino swimming
    As little Sim had said.

In the white morning sunlight
    It looked so very striking –
Its figurehead and rudder
    Like the vessel of a Viking.

But that it swam for love and peace
    And never swam for war
Was clear as was the water
    About that trinosaur.

And through the river-valley
    They watched the trino go,
And up above the trees its head
    Move gently to and fro.

'Such beauty,' said His Worship,
  'It makes me feel so tearful.
Now why did we all think the *she*
  So frightening and fearful?

'Although it broke up floors and doors
  And sheds and beds and ceilings,
It's clearer now – one should allow
  For trinos' FINER FEELINGS.

'In all the world it's certain,
  Few creatures have such charm,
And – come to think of it – it did
  No-one the SLIGHTEST harm.'

(To hear them talking you'd have thought
  That every mother's son
Was eager to have trino two
  As well as trino one.)

But observations of this kind
  Were rapidly cut short
When from afar there came a Sound
  Of Sinister Import.

They heard loud squeals from tyres and wheels
   On missiles quite appalling,
And Non-Commissioned Officers
   A-bellowing and bawling.

All up and down the steeps the jeeps
Were hooting and were humming,
And trucks and lorries by the score
Gave many a rattle and a roar
As if to say,
               'O trinosaur
The Army's
     coming
       COMING.'

They'd umpteen different kinds of gun
And ammunition by the ton
Including bomb and shell and mine
And booby-traps of dread design,
And, camouflaged in blue and green,
Of aspect menacing and mean,
The very first one ever seen,

A military submarine

108

That for the trino would have done
As soon as battle had begun,
Had not the citizens insisted
That it was time the troops DESISTED
From all their plans the beast to KILL
(It made the people feel quite ill) –

So, quite spontaneously,

'NO!'

They cried,

'Now let that trino GO!

Destroy it?

Why,
No thought's absurder.
It's nothing more nor less than murder!
A crime's how history would construe it,
We CANNOT let the Army do it,
For though it came – and this we stress –
In ANSWER to our S.O.S.,
(And to have done so's VERY kind)
We've had a sudden change of mind.

Shake 24

'Far better,'
         they said,
               'that we help if we can
The trino to live out its natural span,
And not out of malice or simply for sport
Its life here on earth for a second cut short.
The soldiers will think we are greener than grass
If all we can think of is,
                  "THEY SHALL NOT PASS!"
(Such slogans would seem to them terribly rum
For, if you remember, WE ASKED them to COME).

'Yes, it's clear as the sign on the side of a bus
A trino's a place on this planet – like us,
And all of a sudden it's plain as can be
It's part of creation, like you and like me.

'WE COULDN'T expose it (too painful the topic!)
To gaggles of gunners with sights telescopic.
It'd scare the poor creature clean out of its wits
If the Royal Artillery blew it to bits.
So let's go together to Watergate Street,
And try and persuade it to beat a retreat.'

The folk to the river then ran in a throng

To the spot where the trino was swimming along –
A picture so peaceful of primeval bliss
As it waved its head happily that way and this.

But seeing the crowd that appeared on the verge
It put on its brakes and prepared to submerge
(A move, come to think of it, childish and callow –
The river just here was decidedly shallow),

And what with the people, including the Mayor,
All leaping,
      and pointing,
           and shouting,

    'TAKE CARE!'

The trinosaur, looking a trifle perplexed,
Seemed rather uncertain as what to do next,
And in its sad eyes two great tears seemed to quiver
As if to say,
              'WHY
                      are they pointing down-river
With stick and umbrella and finger and thumb?
How VERY unfriendly –
                          I've only just come –
If you're cross that I'm late –
                              Well, I caught the first tide–
And ALL that I'm seeking's a trinosaur bride.'

With fears for its safety now seaward they pointed,
The whole river-bank with directions anointed,
Waved SHEETS on which ARROWS they'd
    HASTILY PAINTED
That with its escape-route the beast was acquainted –

When, loud as a thunder-stroke, clear as a flash,

Right into its brain-box

        their message
          fell
            CRASH:

And it turned
      ROUNDABOUT
            with a whirl and a splash,
And soon beyond range of the shells and the shots
It swam for the sea at a fast rate of knots,
First pausing to give to the crowd on the banks
    A nod of its head just as if to say
        thanks.

Then up to the town ran the folk from the creek,
  Delighted the trino was saved – by a squeak;
And puffing and bluffing (and hiding a grin)

They waved and they cheered as the Army came in.

'Good day,' said the General. 'Jolly bad show.
  Leave that tiresome trino to us, doncherknow.'

But O with a charmingly innocent air,
  'Better never than late,' said His Worship the Mayor.

Some other Puffins

THE SEA IS SINGING

Rosalind Kerven

Tess lives right in the north of Scotland, in the Shetland Islands, and when she starts hearing the weird and eerie singing from the sea it is her neighbour, old Jacobina Tait, who helps her understand it. With her strange talk of whales and 'patterns' Jacobina makes Tess realize that she cannot – and must not ignore what the singing is telling her. But how can Tess decipher the message?

RACSO AND THE RATS OF NIMH

Jane Leslie Conly

When fieldmouse Timothy Frisby rescues young Racso, the city rat, from drowning, it's the beginning of a friendship. It's also the beginning of Racso's education – and an adventure. For the two are caught up in the brave and resourceful struggle of the Rats of NIMH to save Thorn Valley, their home, from destruction.

A TASTE OF BLACKBERRIES

Doris Buchanan Smith

The moving story about a young boy who has to come to terms with the tragic death of his best friend and the guilty feeling that he could somehow have saved him.

STAN

Ann Pilling

Running away from his London foster home, Stan unwittingly gets caught up with vicious criminals and is pursued by one of them. But throughout his terrifying journey to Warrington and Liverpool and then by ferry across the Irish Sea, he never loses the hope or the determination to find his brother and the home he dreams of.

TORCH

Jill Paton Walsh

Dio and Cal had gone to ask the old man for permission to marry. Instead, Dio finds himself commanded to be the Guardian of the Torch in the old man's stead. Without quite knowing why, they embark on an extraordinary journey, bearing the Torch in search of the Games! And in doing so they learn some of the secrets of the Torch and of the mysterious past time called 'Ago', a time of wonderful machines, now lost for ever.

CRUMMY MUMMY AND ME

Anne Fine

How would you feel if your mother had royal-blue hair and wore lavender fishnet tights? It's not easy for Minna being the only sensible one in the family, even though she's used to her mum's weird clothes and eccentric behaviour. But then the whole family are a bit unusual and their exploits make highly entertaining reading.

BOSS OF THE POOL

Robin Klein

The last thing Shelley wanted was to have to spend her evenings at the hostel where her mother worked, because she wasn't allowed to stay in the house on her own. Then to her horror, mentally-handicapped Ben attaches himself to her and although he's terrified of the pool, he comes to watch her swimming. Despite herself, Shelley begins to help him overcome his fear. A compassionate story of the growth of an unlikely friendship.

MATILDA

Roald Dahl

Matilda is an extraordinary girl, sensitive and brilliant. But her parents are gormless, and think Matilda is just a nuisance and treat her as a scab, to be endured until the time comes to flick her away. As if this isn't enough, she has to cope with the odious headmistress, Miss Trunchbull. When Matilda is attacked by Miss Trunchbull one day, she suddenly discovers she has an extraordinary power which can make trouble for the monstrous grown-ups in her life.

NOW THEN, CHARLIE ROBINSON

Sylvia Woods

Charlie Robinson is always full of ideas, whether he's trying to liven up a maths lesson, solve the mystery of noises up a chimney or turn the Nativity Play into a really special event. His exploits at home, at school and out and about in the village make very entertaining reading.